THE SILENT MOUNTAIN MAN

MOVIN' TO THE MOUNTAINS
BOOK 1

CASEY COX

ABOUT THE BOOK

Nearly getting killed in a mudslide only reminds me why I hate the mountains. I'm uninjured, but my car is wrecked, there's no way I can get into town, and of course there's no reception here.

I'm screwed.

Maybe it's karma for putting this trip off. I haven't been able to bring myself to visit since Pa's funeral.

And then there are the painful memories that still haunt me of my first love...and first heartbreak.

The summer I turned eighteen, I exchanged letters with a free-spirited, long-haired boy who lived down the road from my father. We hung out all day and wrote each other romantic letters all night. It was the best time of my life.
But now they're both gone, and I'm all alone.

Literally. This mountain feels deserted. Like I'm the only living soul on it.

And then, just as I'm about to give up all hope, a pickup truck pulls up. A man steps out.

Not just any man, though... Pure. Mountain man. Perfection. Big muscles, a thick beard just begging to be touched, and an intense stare that's making me rethink my dislike of the mountains.

Harrick offers me a place to stay, and despite being a total stranger, there's something familiar about him that makes me feel like I can trust him. Also, what other choice have I got?

He takes me back to his cabin. Turns out, he's not much of a talker. I can work with that.

We hook up. I can *definitely* work with that.

I almost forget that I'm here to sell my father's house and finally move on from the guy who left me brokenhearted all those years ago.

And then I find a letter in Harrick's house—one of the letters I wrote all those years ago—and *everything* changes.

Dear Emo Bastard,

Meet me at midnight. Same spot as last time.

I've got something ~~importa~~ to tell you.

Princess

1

Eddie

I hate the mountains.

Despise them.

I could quite happily live the rest of my life without setting foot anywhere near or on one ever again.

And I've never hated the mountains as much as I do right now.

"This is bad," I mutter, gripping the steering wheel with ghost-white knuckles. No matter how hard I squint, I'm barely able to see anything through the intense rainstorm engulfing me.

"This is *real* bad."

It's been raining on and off for most of the drive up the mountain, but it's really bucketing down now.

Is this how I die?

I've only just turned twenty-seven and have finally, *finally*, started to get my shit together. Dream job. Nice apartment. Made the final loan repayment on my car last month.

Why does my life have to end now?

I can already picture the headlines: *Eddie Boyd joins the 27 club.*

Okay, so I'm not a musician, artist, actor, or some other celebrity, but that doesn't mean I can't be the first hotshot marketing exec. to get admitted, right? I spearheaded the *Barbie* movie campaign rollout in Europe. I convinced Taylor Swift to promote collagen-infused bubbly water drinks in Japan. There is literally no club or bar I can't get into in LA or New York.

But do I really want to use my charming smile and ability to talk under water to get me into the big club in the sky?... No, I very much do not.

The rain eases off a fraction. Not a whole lot, but enough to give me a chance to take a few deep breaths and try to compose myself.

I'm crawling at twenty miles an hour, but there's no one else stupid enough to be out on the road so it doesn't matter. There's no way I'm going any faster and risking careening over the edge of the mountain.

That's it. I've decided.

I am *not* dying today.

27 club, you can go fuck yourself.

I continue inching my way up the winding road.

Guess the bad weather is my karma for delaying this trip for as long as I have. I've come up with every excuse I can to avoid coming back here.

My father died a few months ago, and this is my first time back since his funeral. He left me his house and all his worldly belongings. It's time to sell his place. I guess I'll have to sort through all his stuff and decide what to keep, what to give away, and what to throw out. I'm not really sure what the playbook for dealing with the aftermath of your estranged father's death is.

All I know is, I *so* don't want to be doing this.

Growing up, I used to love Pa more than anyone. Mom would drop me off at the start of summer, and he'd take me hiking, fishing, teach me how to start a fire by rubbing sticks together like they do in the movies, show me which berries were safe to eat and which weren't.

All my best childhood memories are from here, from this place, from him...

Until the summer I turned eighteen and everything went to shit. My whole world got turned upside down. It's taken me *years* to recover.

A deep, earth-shaking rumble rattles the car. I peer up at the dark-gray sky. "That wasn't thunder."

Yes, I'm a talker.

No, I don't require an audience.

An ominous feeling washes over me. "If that *wasn't* thunder, what the hell was it?"

The rainstorm reintensifies, pellets of water slamming down onto the car so hard the entire vehicle shakes.

And the *noise*. It's so freaking loud I can barely hear myself think. The wipers are going full force, but it's not making much of a difference. I can't see shit.

Another rumble.

Louder this time.

Closer.

And then...a blistering crack, and the car jolts.

"Fuck! What is happening?"

I slam on the brakes.

But just because the car has stopped, doesn't mean I'm not moving.

I am.

Back and forth, back and forth, like I'm a baby being rocked to sleep by a junkie on meth.

Something is very, *very* wrong.

And then, out of the blue, I get an impulse.

A crazy, stupid impulse.

Potentially the wildest impulse I've ever gotten.

I don't overthink it. Like I do in my career, I go with my gut. And for whatever reason, my gut is screaming at me to get the fuck out of the vehicle.

I yank off my seat belt, grab my phone from the center console, and jump out of my car.

I'm instantly drenched, the warm rain is falling down hard, turning my white shirt translucent as it sticks to my body.

But my intuition isn't done yet.

Move!

I start backing away from the car, slowly at first, until I feel a rumble all the way down into my bones.

That sound, that feeling, that's not thunder... It's a freaking mudslide.

I look up. "Holy fucking shit!"

Not wasting another second, I turn and run as fast as I can.

I'm almost past the first bend in the road when there's an almighty boom. If I didn't know what was happening, I'd say an explosion went off because that's exactly what it sounds like. Mother Nature sure is letting it rip today.

I turn back around, my eyes widening in horror as a giant chunk of the mountain slides down and buries my car in mud.

The force of so much earth moving shakes the ground beneath my feet. I fall. I try to get back up, but everything is moving so intensely, I can't scramble back onto my feet no matter how hard I try.

So I stop.

Go still.

It's too late to run.

I can't do anything. I have to accept my fate. Maybe today *is* the day Eddie Boyd meets his maker.

27 club, room for one more?

With the ground convulsing underneath me, my life flashes before my eyes.

Summers with Pa.

The first time I scored the lead on a major advertising campaign.

One of the few good birthdays I had, when I was four, maybe five years old, before Mom and Dad split up.

The rush I got riding my first roller coaster. I freaked out the whole time because I stood on my tippy-toes to make the required height limit, and I was convinced I would fall out and plummet to my death the second we looped upside down.

My first kiss.

I let out a gasp at the memory before an unguarded sob escapes me.

Princess.

That's not his name, but that's what I called him. The free-spirited, long-haired guy who lived down the road from Pa that fateful summer after I graduated from high school.

I was deep in an emo phase, and I went all in. I'm talking

dying my hair black, getting piercings—thanks to a fake ID—wearing nothing but black, the whole shebang.

Whereas Michael, that was his name, was the same age as me, but he was...he was wild and free and gorgeous. With the most incredible smile. Loved an adventure. The only person I've ever met in my whole life who talked more than I did, which is really saying something.

And he had the most intense stare. His eyes would narrow, and it made everything else in the world disappear. I'll never forget it. I'll never forget *him*, and I know that for a fact, because despite years passing, I still think about him. A lot.

He made me feel seen. Like I mattered even though I had no idea who I was or what I wanted to do with the rest of my life.

By that age, I was too old for boy scout adventures with Pa, so I hung out with Michael every day. We'd go swimming in the lake, explore the caves, and one late afternoon, with the sun setting in the distance and our legs dangling off the cliff's edge, I had my first kiss. It was...magical.

And we did this thing, I can't remember who started it, I think it might have been me, actually, but we did this thing where we wrote each other letters and left them in the mailbox for the other one to pick up first thing in the morning.

It may sound schmaltzy and kind of silly, but it wasn't. It was real.

That summer, I had my first love.

Swiftly followed by my first heartbreak.

And *that's* why I hate the mountains.

Not only did I get my heart broken here, I've also never found anyone who's come close to making me feel what Michael did.

Now he's gone, and so is Pa, and I'm all alone.

But I'm... I'm still alive.

I glance around, snapping back to reality. The ground has stopped shaking. "Holy shit, I've survived."

I push myself up to a seated position. My newly paid-off car, along with a good chunk of the mountainside, is gone.

"I can't believe I got out of there."

What was that voice, that feeling, that impulse I had to get the hell out of my car? I have no idea, but it literally saved my life. I'd be a goner if I'd stayed put.

It's still raining, but I've gotten used to it now. I tilt my head back, looking up at the sky, the droplets coming down on my face. "Thanks, God. Owe you one."

I readjust how I'm sitting and notice my cell phone next to me. "And thank god I had the sense to take you with me."

It's as wet as I am, so I do my best to dry it off a little, then unlock it. The screen comes to life, but dammit, there's no reception.

"Because of course there isn't."

I stand up and take a few steps, waving the phone around every which way because everyone knows that's how you get a signal, right?

It's no use. Reception on the mountain has always been patchy at best, and I'm not even anywhere near the small town of Thickehead.

I'm shit out of luck, that's what I am.

No car. No cellphone. No human soul around for miles.

I shiver. I'm also saturated and starting to get cold. The warm rain doesn't feel so warm anymore. I rub my wet hands up and down my wet arms but it does nothing to heat me up.

"Great. All I need now is for some crazy serial killer to show up and chop me up into pieces."

And right on cue, an old-school red pickup truck comes into view.

I shake my fist at the angry-looking sky. "I was kidding. Come on. Give me a break."

The truck gets closer. My heart starts thumping. This could be really bad. I'm all alone out here with no way of calling for help or escaping. If whoever is in that pickup is bad news, I'm done for.

The vehicle comes to a stop about thirty feet away from me.

Panic shoots through me, but what can I do? I can't run. The wreckage caused by the mudslide is behind me, and the vehicle is blocking the only way out.

I could scream, but who'd hear me?

The door opens.

A pair of black boots hits the ground.

I start open-mouth breathing, my mind racing with all sorts of nightmare scenarios.

Note to future self should I make it out of this alive: stop watching serial killer documentaries on Netflix before long road trips. My already overactive imagination doesn't need the extra help.

The person, a man, steps out from behind the door and into view. I almost choke on the rain.

He's not just any man. He's pure mountain man perfection.

The rain soaks him in a few seconds, causing his red-and-black flannel shirt to mold to his perfectly sculpted chest, broad shoulders, and big biceps. He's left the top few buttons of his shirt undone, revealing a hint of hair and golden skin.

He swipes a hand through his long, wavy, and now wet dark-brown hair, causing his bicep to flex. That's when I notice his thick, veiny forearms.

"Universe, you are really testing me today," I murmur under my breath.

I can't recall when or where it started, but I have a thing for veiny forearms...as well as *other* veiny appendages. It just... works for me, okay?

He starts walking toward me. "What are you doing out here?"

His deep voice cuts through the rain.

"Oh, you know, just enjoying the view."

He doesn't say anything, but he stops walking. His eyes rake over me, and it's like they have hands because I swear I can *feel* his gaze gliding over my wet skin.

His dark eyes narrow, and for a split second, I get struck by a sense of déjà vu. Not of having experienced this moment before, because, hello, I think I'd remember, but of *him*.

Which is impossible, because I'd also definitely remember if I'd ever run into this mountain of a man before.

He brings his hands to his hips, and lord almighty, the effortless masculine swagger he exudes makes my core clench.

Maybe the mountains aren't so bad after all?

"Where's your car?"

I point to the big pile of sludge behind me. "Somewhere in there."

"I see."

His eyes make their way back to me. He looks me up and down. Shamelessly. Not even trying to be discreet.

And I'm...not mad about it.

Which is crazy. I should be mad. Or at least slightly worried. Just because the guy is hot as fuck doesn't mean he can't hurt me. He's taller and bigger than me. I have no idea who he is. I don't even know his name. And we're out in the wilderness, miles away from civilization.

But the part of the brain that goes into self-preservation mode when you think you're about to die must be located next to the part of the brain responsible for extreme horniness, because instead of planning my next move for survival—*which would be the smart thing to do*—all I can think about is what it would be like to have this muscular mountain man touching me, kissing me, *fucking me senseless.*

Yep. I haven't been laid in a *looong* time. Guess it's starting to mess with my head. Both of them.

"Come on," the guy says, waving a hand and heading back to his truck.

"Um, excuse me. What?"

He turns around, a wry smile on his face. "You're coming back to my place."

2

Harrick

"Like fuck I am. I'm not going *anywhere* with you. I don't even know you."

"Got a better offer?"

"Well, no, but, but... You could be a serial killer."

"I'm not a serial killer."

"That's *exactly* what a serial killer would say."

I bite back the smile brewing on my lips. He really doesn't have any other option, but I decide to go along with it. By the looks of things, he's lucky to have made it out of the mudslide alive. It's understandable he'd be a little on edge right now.

"My name is Harrick, and I'm twenty-eight years old. I live in Brackenridge, and I'm a..." My throat constricts. "I'm a military vet."

Man, I haven't spoken this many words all month.

He folds his arms across his chest, his expression remaining suspicious.

"And why were you driving this way?"

"To get supplies."

"To murder people?"

"No. To eat."

"People?"

"Food."

He rubs his chin, like he's seriously thinking about it. Geez, I know I don't exactly give off welcoming committee vibes, but am I that much of an ogre that this guy is seriously weighing up whether or not I murder people? Or eat them?

Maybe I am.

I moved back to the mountains after my third tour. I needed to get away from people. To try to move on and live a simple life, to forget all the things I saw while serving. *Like my best friend bleeding out in my arms...*

"I'm Eddie."

The words jolt me out of my head.

"Nice to meet you, *Eddie*."

That name...

"Yeah. You too, Harrick."

"Come on. Let's go before we both catch a cold."

I turn and make my way back to my pickup. A few seconds later, I hear footsteps behind me. I get into my truck and watch as Eddie ambles over, taking his sweet-ass time. He's probably still unsure if this is the right thing to do, but he's safe with me. I won't hurt him.

I knew an Eddie once. He was my first love. But he left me without saying a word, disappeared in the middle of the night, and I never saw or heard from him ever again.

Another good reason to live up here. The only two men I've ever cared about aside from my brothers—my best friend and my first love—have both left me.

People only bring pain. Living alone is a much better option. Yeah, it's lonely, but it beats getting hurt.

Eddie reaches the passenger-side door. He takes a deep breath before opening it and climbing into the cabin.

I fumble around in the back seat to find a towel. "Here."

"Thanks."

He takes it from me and smiles, then starts drying off his hair.

He looks nothing like my Eddie.

This Eddie has got sandy-blond hair, blue eyes that sparkle like the ocean, and thanks to the white T-shirt that's gone translucent in the rain, I can see he's got a smooth, lean body. Not a piercing in sight.

Unlike my Eddie. He was pierced all over.

I wonder what brings this Eddie to these parts. He's most likely a tourist. Thickehead attracts plenty of those. It's a cute little town with cobblestone streets, filled with restaurants, a buttload of breweries, inns, shops, and good people...if you're into that sort of thing.

It's too much activity for me. I live on the other side of the mountain where it's totally secluded and only make my way into town every few weeks to stock up on supplies.

Eddie finishes drying off and hands the towel back to me. I run it down one arm at a time. He tracks the movement, his tongue poking out the side of his mouth. I'd say he was checking me out, but I bet he's probably still wondering if I go around murdering people for fun. I finish up and throw the towel into the back seat.

"Check the glove compartment," I tell him.

"Okay." He opens it then gasps. "What the fuck is that?"

"It's a gun."

"I know it's a fucking gun. I can see that. What are you going to do with that?"

"Nothing. It's for you. I want you to feel safe."

He slams the glove compartment shut, keeping his hands on it. "Okay. So here's the thing about me. I don't like guns. Or the mountains. I'm a city boy through and through. I mean, I used to come up here for the summers and spend them with my dad..."

I start the truck and head back to my place while Eddie regales me with the story of summers spent in the mountains with his father, which eventually morphs into the reason why he's here now.

"Pa died five months ago."

"I'm sorry for your loss. It sounds like you two were close."

"*Were* being the operative word." He looks out the window and lets out a long breath. "It's a long story. Complicated. Anyway, he left me his house in his will, so I've come back to sell it. That is, before the weather decided to fuck with me, and I almost died."

He loosens his seat belt and turns so he's facing me. "Thank you for rescuing me. Not in an *I'm a Disney princess and need to be saved by a hot mountain man* way, but, like, I'd be seriously screwed if you hadn't shown up."

"Yeah. You would be." I flick my eyes over to him for a second and smirk. "You realize you just called me hot."

He smiles. "Is it really that much of a shock?"

I shrug a shoulder.

"Oh, come on. You're a freaking mountain god. Tall, muscly, your beard is perfection, and don't even get me started on your forearms."

I lift my left hand off the steering wheel for a second and peer down at my arm. "Forearms?"

"Yeah. Hello." He reaches over and traces the tip of his index finger along a vein.

A wolfish grin hits my lips. "You like that?"

"Uh-huh." He pulls his hand back. "I swear I'm not some kinky sex freak or anything."

"So it's established then," I say seriously.

"What's established?"

"That I'm not a serial killer, and you're not a kinky sex freak."

"Hmm, maybe."

"Which part are you maybe-ing about?"

Eddie starts laughing. Loudly. It surprises me, mainly because I'm not the kind of person who makes people laugh. I'm so distracted I have to hit the brakes a little harder than I want to in order to make the turnoff.

"Sorry." I apologize for the rough turn.

"It's fine."

And his laugh. There's something about that laugh. Almost as if I've heard it before...

No. That's impossible. I've never met this guy. Although, for a complete stranger, he sure has a knack for getting me to talk. And crack jokes. Gonna need to buy some throat lozenges if I keep yacking away at this rate.

I'm just trying to put him at ease, I tell myself. Once we're safe and sound in my cabin, I'll revert back to my usual quiet ways.

Besides, I already get the feeling he's a talker, which suits me just fine.

"This is your place?" Eddie asks ten minutes later as I pull up out the front of my log cabin.

"Yep."

"Wow. It's so pretty. Like something you'd see in the movies," he says as we both get out of the truck.

I make my way next to him. "Pretty?"

"Yeah." He pokes my side with his elbow. "For a serial killer's house."

I shake my head. "Come on. Let's get inside."

The rain has let up a bit, but we're both soaked to the bone. I open the front door, and we step inside.

"You don't lock your door?"

"No need to, City Boy."

His elbow makes contact with my stomach this time.

Eddie looks around from the entryway. "I like your place."

"This is basically it."

I point at the open-plan kitchen, living, and dining area in front of us. There's not much to it, but I'm proud of it. I built it myself using reclaimed wood from my brother's timber yard.

Eddie's eyes go wide. "Oh my god, you have a fireplace."

"I do."

"I *looove* watching a fire. It's one of my favorite things."

It's one of my favorite things, too.

But I don't say that. Instead, I take a step away from Eddie, feeling...*unsettled* for some reason.

"Bathroom's that way." I tip my head to the small hallway that leads to the bathroom and my bedroom. "Go jump in the shower. I'll get you a towel and a set of clothes and leave them by the door."

"Yeah. Okay. Just gonna lock myself up in some strange mountain dude's bathroom."

I'm about to remind him he has a gun at his disposal when he lifts a finger, and his lips stretch out. "I'm teasing."

It takes every ounce of willpower I can muster not to grab his finger, pull him into me, and wipe that sexy smile off his lips with a kiss...but I don't.

"Go," I instruct.

He bounces down the hall, and my eyes absorb the hard muscles of his back and a round, pert ass that does little to quell the desire coursing through my veins.

I'm attracted to the guy. That much is obvious. But I can't, *won't*, do anything about it. Not when I'm trying to get him to trust me and make him feel comfortable after what he's been through.

I'll take care of my libido the way I always do. Alone.

The shower starts running, so I grab Eddie a towel and some clothes he can change into.

What a funny coincidence that, of all the names in the world, his happens to be Eddie.

My Eddie made me feel so many things.

Back then, I was capable of having emotions. And talking. Fuck, I was a chatterbox. You couldn't shut me up. And believe me, my two older brothers tried to.

I wasn't the jaded, damaged, silent emotionless ice block I've turned into. Life hadn't worn me down yet.

Not that growing up was easy, especially not with the kind of father we had, but it was always an adventure. I had so much energy. So much passion about everything. I was bursting with excitement about the future.

Our future.

And it all died when Eddie left.

I joined the military a few months later, and I grew the fuck up. I stopped being a boy, shut my mouth once and for all, and stepped out of my father's shadow.

I chose a different life. A proper life. One that didn't involve being on the run all the time, never staying in one place for too long, always checking over my shoulder and making sure no one ever got too close.

The army was just the thing I needed. It gave me the discipline and structure I'd been missing. I finally became a man I could be proud of.

I rummage through my clothes, looking for something that will fit this Eddie. He's shorter than me, so I pick out the smallest shirt and sweatpants I have. I fold them neatly and place them, and the towel, by the bathroom door.

I can hear Eddie singing a My Chemical Romance song, which I know but can't remember the name of, in the shower. That's gotta be a good sign. He wouldn't be belting out a tune if he really thought his life was in danger, would he?

I head back into the living room and throw a few logs onto the fire. It starts crackling away, and I stare into it, remembering all the times my Eddie and I would sit around a fire. We could have easily let the evening drift into night and spend hours talking, but his father was strict about curfew for some reason and always insisted Eddie be back home by seven.

Another funny coincidence, both Eddies call their dads Pa.

I look down the hall, to the thin strip of light peeking through from under the bathroom door. "You're being a fool," I scold myself. "That's not your Eddie. Are you crazy, man?"

My Eddie was a full-on emo. He had jet-black hair and brown eyes, piercings all over. He looked nothing like this guy.

He'd told me that the emo thing was a phase. That if I'd met him a summer earlier, I wouldn't recognize him. That he'd been picking and choosing different personas since he was fourteen, trying to find the right one. The one that fit.

I was able to see past his ripped clothes and angst. I saw him. Who he really was. A good person, a beautiful soul, trying to figure shit out, just like the rest of us.

Until he fucking disappeared without so much as a word... or even a letter.

The shower stops. A few moments later, the door opens a crack. I turn away to give Eddie some privacy, and when I look next, the door's closed and the clothes and towel are gone.

The fire's roaring now. I'm standing close enough to it that it's drying me off a little. S'pose I should go pick out some clothes for myself, too.

As I make my way to my bedroom, my mind drifts back to that summer ten years ago, and to the first letter I found in my mailbox...

Dear Michael,

I have a confession to make.

One I can't bring myself to tell you in person. I'm loving spending time with you, and I don't want to mess it up. If I write it in a letter, I won't see your face if you get mad at me.

I really hope you don't get mad at me.

Okay, so my confession is...your name is kinda weird.

There's nothing wrong with the name itself, it's just that, well... you're not a Michael. You don't look like a Michael, or behave like one, either.

Michaels have short hair. They're responsible. They return their library books on time. They get good but not great grades. They have younger sisters who they say they don't like but they'd protect and do anything for.

I don't know why, but I'm not getting Michael vibes from you.

Do you hate me? Please don't hate me.

EB

Dear Eddie,

There's a few things to unpack here.

Firstly, you do realize you could've asked me for my number, and we could be texting each other? What's with the letter? Not that I mind. It's cute...in a retro, time-warp kind of way.

EB? I'm assuming they're your initials. What's your last name?

Speaking of names, no I'm not offended. You actually busted me. Michael is a fake name I'm using in Thickehead. My dad's actually a low-level criminal, so he, my brothers, and I move around a lot. I never tell anyone my real name.

Funny coincidence: I picked Michael for all the reasons you mentioned.

What would you prefer to call me?

Mich—Nope, I'll leave that up to you.

PS - I think you're really beautiful.

3

Eddie

I swipe the fogged-up bathroom mirror with my hand to get a proper look at myself.

"Yep, just as I suspected."

I am *drowning* in Harrick's clothes. I look like a kid who's inherited his way older brother's hand-me-downs.

On the plus side, they smell nice, so there's that.

And since I don't really have any other choice but to wear what I've been given, I hand brush my curls to try to tame them —it doesn't work, it never does—take one final look at myself in the mirror, and head out.

Harrick's standing by the fire, holding what I assume is a change of clothes. He's still wet, his jeans and shirt sculpted perfectly to his masculine body, his hair flat and damp.

"Bathroom's free."

He looks up. His eyes narrow just a fraction, and for a split second, my breath escapes me. *Those eyes...* There's something about those eyes.

He clears his throat with a grunt, and when he walks past and locks his gaze on me, the air between us sizzles.

"Make yourself at home," he mutters before shutting the bathroom door.

"All right." I glance around the living room. "What have we got here?"

A nice, rustic mountain cabin by the looks of things. The place is decorated simply, which is kind of nice. My place back home looks like a tornado tore through it. Harrick doesn't have a lot of stuff, but everything is neat and tidy.

There's a large two-seater facing the fireplace, a bookcase that's more empty than it is filled with books, and a small rectangular dining table with some folders and papers arranged neatly in one corner.

I walk over to the fire and bury my toes in the plush sheepskin rug. I stretch my hands out toward the flames, warming my palms.

I wiggle my fingers. The same fingers that reached out and touched Harrick's veiny forearm in the pickup.

He didn't pull away or tell me not to touch him. Couple that with the unmistakable way he's been checking me out, and I'm ninety-nine percent sure he's gay and possibly interested.

I'm also ninety-nine percent confident he's not a serial killer.

Which all adds up to: I'm most likely not going to get killed, and I could end up getting some good mountain dick. I smile to myself. I always liked math at school.

"You good?"

I jump. "Shit. You scared me. You done already?"

"Mhmm." Harrick walks over to the kitchen and opens the refrigerator. "You hungry? Thirsty?"

I eye him up, bent over with his perfect muscular ass on fine display in his tight black sweatpants.

I wasn't, but I am now.

He pops his head around the side of the door and looks at me, a long strand of brown hair falling across his face. He tucks it behind his ear.

"A glass of water would be great."

He nods, fills two glasses, and joins me on the couch.

"Thanks," I say, taking it from him.

His intense eyes never leave me. He's got the kind of eyes that make you wonder what's going on behind them.

What's he thinking?

What's he thinking about *me*?

Apart from me being a hot mess who almost got killed in a mudslide, has called him a serial killer multiple times, and inadvertently called him hot when I was talking nonstop on the way back to his place... And there I go answering my own question.

I put my glass down carefully on the wooden floor since Harrick doesn't have a coffee table. "I have an idea. Let's get to know each other better."

Harrick takes a sip of water, but doesn't say anything.

"All right. I'll go first. What would you like to know about me?"

I swear if water was chewable, he'd be chewing the ever-loving life out of the mouthful of it he's got.

"Okay. I'll just start rambling, and you tell me when to stop. Deal?"

Our eyes meet. A tiny smile surfaces on his lips. "Deal."

"Well, you already know my name, what I'm doing in the mountains, and the fate that befell my poor little Corolla. Let's see." I drum my fingers against my thigh. "What else can I tell you about myself?"

"I also know you like a good forearm flex." As he says it, he lifts his arm and makes a fist, the veins in his forearm popping like crazy.

Heat warms my cheeks. "You remember."

He drops his arm and drapes it over the back of the sofa. "As if I'd forget that."

"So, okay, yes, I have that little thing. Which is a nice segue to, okay, yes, I'm gay."

Our eyes lock. I'm studying him for any signs of a response, positive or negative. I get nothing apart from that full-on stare of his.

Okay. So he's not very talkative *and* hard to read. Looks like I'll be the one doing the legwork then. "Are you gay?"

"I am."

"Cool. And are you...single?"

"I am."

I reach over, pick up my glass, and guzzle down some water. "That's...great."

I don't know what it is about Harrick, but he unnerves me. Not in a bad way, just in a way I'm not used to. I've met celebrities, politicians, powerful businesspeople, and yet no one's ever turned my head to mush like this before. Sure, I've been starstruck, but this is something else entirely.

"So, back to me telling you a bit about myself. Let's see... I'm twenty-seven. I'm a marketing executive for a leading entertainment agency. And..."

My age and my job? That's the best I can come up with? Why am I not describing myself better? I'm a pretty interesting person. I've been to a ton of places. I know how to scuba dive. I speak okay-ish Spanish. Despite leaving my heavy emo phase in my angsty teenage years where it belongs, I can still sing every My Chemical Romance song ever.

Normally, I can talk underwater. What is going on with me today?

I flick my gaze over to the fire burning brightly. Some of the tension instantly melts away. Don't know what it is, but staring into the flames always relaxes me. Some time passes before I hear, "You okay?"

I turn my head toward Harrick. "Yeah. I'm good. Sorry if I'm acting...flighty. I'm usually a lot better with words."

"No need to apologize," he says, his voice dropping into husky territory.

Our eyes meet again. A torrent of heat bursts in my chest. I'm struggling with words, so maybe I should switch to something that doesn't involve talking?

I lick my lips and reach my hand out. As if he knows exactly what I'm wanting to do, Harrick mirrors the movement, lifting his arm closer to me.

My fingertips graze his forearm, skimming the smooth skin on the underside, then finding a vein and tracing over it.

His dark eyes fall to my lips.

I shuffle closer to him.

He doesn't move.

I move a little more. Then some more.

By my third shuffle, the sides of our legs are touching.

I look up at him. "You gonna make me do *all* the work?"

"No." His eyes go soft. "Only wanted to make sure you feel safe and comfortable and that this is really what you want."

"This is really what I want," I whisper.

"You sure?"

My breath trembles as I stare into his dark eyes. "I am."

"Because I have to tell you, that once I start fucking you, Eddie, *I'll* be the one doing all the work. I'll be the one making sure you feel better than you've ever felt before. Is that what you want?"

Fuck to the yes yes yes! "It is."

Harrick smirks, and in one swift move, his lips are on mine. I close my eyes as he wraps an arm around my waist and tugs me even closer to him. My hands land on his round shoulders, and I let out a small gasp at how solid they are.

He eases his tongue into my mouth, the tips of our noses touching gently. I can smell his shower wash on him.

And on me.

Our mouths merge, and the kiss deepens.

My cock aches in my pants, swelling with desire as I slide my hands up Harrick's neck until I finally reach the holy grail—his sexy-as-fuck beard. It's softer than it looks, and my fingers melt right into it.

Harrick growls in approval as I stroke his beard, taking me more forcefully with his mouth. He knows how to kiss. In fact, he almost kisses as well as—

My eyes open, and I pull back sharply.

"Everything okay," he asks, his eyes narrowing as he assesses me.

Harrick isn't Michael, my subconscious chides me, but I can't deny that for a brief second, I got my wires crossed, and the thought did pop into my head.

Talk about ludicrous.

For starters, they look nothing alike—Michael had long, dirty-blond hair and was lean—not to mention, hello, he had a different freaking name. Even if Michael wasn't his real name.

What is wrong with me? Maybe surviving a near-death experience has shaken me up more than I realized?

"Sorry. I'm fine," I say, shaking my head and latching on to his rock-solid shoulders again. "I just need a good hard fuck. It's been a while."

Harrick keeps staring at me, and I wonder if he can tell I'm holding something back. He can't. He doesn't know me. He's not in my head. But still...he looks as if he knows I'm hiding something.

"Been a while for me, too. If you want to stop, at any time for any reason, you just tell me, okay?"

I nod. "I will."

"Good."

He smiles, and then before I know what's happening, he stands, scoops me into his arms, and carries me over to the sheepskin rug by the fire.

He places me down gently on it, then undresses me, his attention switching every few seconds between the clothes he's removing and my face.

I take a few deep breaths. I don't know why or how Harrick has stirred up memories of Princess. Maybe it's not even Harrick, maybe just being in the mountains is enough to take me back there.

But how much longer am I going to keep doing this for? It's been over a decade. Why am I still stuck on someone from so long ago? Someone who didn't fight for me. Someone who never even bothered to find me when I was taken away in the middle of the night.

I've spent so much time since that summer trying to find someone who makes me feel even half of what Princess made me feel, when maybe what I really need is a hot encounter with a guy I'll never see again to reset me. A one-night stand is about the only thing I haven't tried to get over Michael.

The past is the past. Pa is gone. Princess is gone. But Harrick is here. And I am beyond ready to leave the pain behind and move on with my life.

Harrick has completely undressed me, and I'm lying here naked on the rug, with his hungry eyes roaming over my naked body. I'm defenseless and completely exposed, and yet, I have this complete sense of safety with this man who I've known for barely a few hours.

Why do I feel so safe with him...?

"You're so beautiful," he whispers reverently. "Anyone ever tell you that?"

I squeeze my eyes shut, trying *not* to think of Princess. He used to tell me that all the time.

"No." I'm unable to bring myself to open my eyes and lie straight to Harrick's face.

Silence follows, and then his lips nudge against my hip bone, his warm breath tickling my delicate skin.

I open my eyes and peer down. Harrick licks my hip, then nibbles a trail of kisses from my hip bone across to my belly button, then up my chest, leaning over toward my left pec.

He stops kissing me. "Oh."

"What is it?"

He frowns deeply, studying my left nipple.

"I used to have my nipple pierced," I explain. "That's what those little marks are. Nothing to be worried about."

"Right."

His eyes flick over to my right nipple.

"Had that one pierced, too," I say.

He turns his head toward my dick. "And I had a Prince Albert."

"I see."

Something about how seriously he's taking this makes me laugh. I don't even know why.

Harrick's gaze cuts to mine. His eyes are blazing. He takes

stock of my naked body one more time, and then he's on top of me, kissing me like his life depends on it.

I asked for a good fuck, and I have a feeling I'm about to get one.

4

Harrick

My head's playing tricks me on. That's gotta be it. There's no other reasonable explanation for it.

I slide my tongue into Eddie's mouth, my hands running up and down his smooth, lean torso.

Sure, the coincidences are piling up—his name, *Pa*, him spending summers up here, and now the piercings he *used* to have—but it's not him.

This Eddie is not *my* Eddie.

But you know what? For this one night we get to spend together, I'm going to pretend that he is. Pretend that my Eddie didn't disappear without a trace all those years ago, and that after that summer, we found a way to be together.

I used to daydream about how we'd start a new life somewhere, away from my father, probably wherever Eddie ended up going to college. He'd gotten accepted into a few places, but hadn't made his final decision yet.

What was it he was planning on studying again? Was it business? Or marketing?

Doesn't this Eddie work in marketing?

Stop it, brain. You're not helping.

But, god, how different my life would've turned out if we'd ended up staying together. I probably wouldn't have joined the military. I was always good with my hands, so I could have gotten a job in construction, worked my ass off, and done everything possible to give Eddie the good life he deserved. Because he was worth it. I would've done anything to make him happy.

And yeah, I would've asked him to marry me one day. Who knows, maybe we could've even had kids...

Cut it out, man.

I've wasted too much time pondering what-ifs. And what's the use? It doesn't change a damn thing, and it only makes me feel like shit. That's the last thing I want to be feeling right now.

Cute, funny, and slightly quirky guys like this Eddie don't exactly fall out of the sky around these parts. This is most likely going to be my one and only time with him before the road reopens and I drive him to Thickehead so he can settle the business he came here to settle.

No more getting distracted by wild ideas. It's time to deliver on my word and give this sexy-as-hell city boy a fucking he'll remember for a lifetime.

I make my way down his body slowly, nibbling and licking his soft, creamy skin as I go, until I reach his cock.

Nothing soft about this.

I curl my fingers around his rigid length and give him a few strokes. His eyes roll into the back of his head. "So good," he groans. "Keep going."

I intend to.

I peel off my shirt and then get into a better position. I hook each of his legs over my shoulders as I lift his lower back off the rug with one hand, giving me the access I need to his sweet hole.

"Jesus," I mutter. "So fucking beautiful."

It really is. His smooth pink hole looks so inviting in the firelight. I waste no more time, holding him up as I dive in between his cheeks. My tongue swipes up his taint, and when I graze his entrance, he squirms in delight.

"Oh god oh god oh god."

I bring two fingers to his pucker, then spread them. Lowering my head again, I pulse my tongue in and out of his small gape, pushing in as far as I can.

I lose track of time after that, but when I'm finally done making out with Eddie's ass, the insides of his cheeks are red from beard rash. I lower him carefully onto the rug.

He crooks a finger. "Come 'ere."

I work my way up his body, tracing a path with my tongue,

finally arriving at his beautiful face. His forehead is sheened with a thin layer of sweat, his eyes alive and sparkling.

"I don't know if they give out Nobel Peace Prizes for eating ass, but they should. Because what you just did to me could end all wars and bring about world peace."

I chuckle. "Don't know about that."

Our eyes meet. Eddie runs his hands into my beard. "That was incredible."

I stare into those dazzling blue orbs, searching for...I don't know what. Confirmation that somehow, against all the odds, he's my Eddie.

I'm being fucking ridiculous. This has to stop.

I clear my throat. "I'm glad you enjoyed the appetizer. You ready for the main course, sir?"

His nails scratch under my beard. "So fucking ready."

"Stay right where you are. Don't move a muscle," I instruct as I get up. "I'll be right back. Gettin' supplies."

I dash into my bedroom and grab the lube and condoms from my bedside drawer. Eddie is where I left him, except he's flipped over and is now on his hands and knees.

Fuck, he's sexy.

He looks over his shoulder and winks. "Oops. I moved a muscle."

I smack the lube bottle into my open palm. "Then I'm afraid you're going to have to be punished."

His lips quirk, and then his gaze drops to the bulge tenting my sweatpants. "With something big, I hope. Otherwise I might not learn my lesson properly."

"Wouldn't want that now, would we?" I drop the supplies onto the rug and take off my sweats.

I smirk. "Big enough for ya?"

Eddie's eyes go huge when they land on my massive cock.

He does a series of little nods. "And so veiny," he whispers breathlessly.

"Not that you're a kinky sex freak, or anything," I tease.

"I'm reconsidering my position on that."

Grinning, I lower myself onto the rug, smear some lube into my hand, and gently press my index finger to his entrance. "Gonna warm you up first."

Eddie is still looking at me over his shoulder. "But only a little. I want to feel this tomorrow."

"We'll see."

I slide a finger into him. He's tight, *really* tight, and despite what he just said, I'm going to need to make sure he's properly stretched out before I take him. Feeling it tomorrow is one thing, hurting him is another.

Slowly, meticulously, one finger becomes two, which soon becomes three.

"I'm ready," Eddie whines, changing position and lying on his back. He spreads his legs. "I am so fucking ready."

Confident that he is, I sheathe my cock, grease it with lube, and align myself to his body. So far, I've managed to stay in control. Set the pace. Slowed him down when he got a little carried away. Made sure he's prepped and ready for me.

But I know that as soon as I enter him, my self-control will snap, and I'm going to fuck him to within an inch of his life. He thinks I'm some big, hot mountain man now, wait until he experiences what I've got in store for him.

I nudge the head of my cock into his channel. Eddie seizes up, his hands gripping my biceps.

"It's okay," I assure him. "I'll go slow."

His throat bobs, then he brings those beautiful eyes to meet mine. "I trust you."

My chest swells with pride, loving hearing those words. For some inexplicable reason, I have this need, this *urge*, to make Eddie feel safe with me. It's been with me from the second I stepped out of my pickup truck and saw him stranded on the side of what was left of the road.

I push a little deeper into him. His eyes flutter closed, and he starts breathing deeply, in through his nose and out through his mouth.

Only once he loosens up a little do I plunge in some more, more, *more*, until finally, I'm fully seated in his luscious warmth.

"Could stay here forever," I murmur. "You feel so good."

"This is heaven," Eddie agrees with a contented sigh. "But now that my ass is used to you, it's hungry. It needs a pounding. Know anyone up for the job?"

"Watch me."

I withdraw my cock until the tip of my crown is at his entrance, then slam my hips into him.

I do the same thing.

Again.

And again.

And again.

Treating him to a series of long, hard, ball-slapping thrusts.

Now *that* shuts him up.

I pick up the pace. It's rare for me to fuck, and it's even rarer to find someone who can take all of me, but it's like Eddie's body was made for me.

I fuck into him with deep, punishing thrusts, and he takes everything I dish out.

He curls his hands around the back of my neck, and we stare at each other, as I drive myself into him, over and over.

He brings a hand to his dick and starts getting himself off.

"Fuck," I growl at the sight. "That's so hot."

"I'm close." He bites his lip. Like he's worried.

"Come for me."

"But I don't want this to be over yet."

"My sweet, silly City Boy." I come to a halt the next time I bottom out, after sinking my entire length hard into him. "If you think you're only coming once tonight, you're sadly mistaken."

I pound into him through his first orgasm...and his second.

Sensing his ass might need a slight reprieve, I coax out his third climax with my mouth.

"I'm spent," he murmurs, as I re-enter his gaping, well-used hole.

"Want me to stop?"

He turns his head, peering up at me over his shoulder. "Stop, and I will murder you."

I snigger. "But what a way to go."

With his channel trained to accommodate me, I waste no time, grabbing a fistful of his hair and surging into him with a rough, uninhibited force.

"Milk that cock with your ass," I growl, pulling his hair.

His back arches. "Fuck, yeah. Didn't picture you as a dirty talker."

Normally, I'm not. But there's something about Eddie...

"Want me to stop?"

"Want to get killed?"

I continue driving into him, my cock spearing into his open, willing hole. I briefly glance down, and my dick disappearing into his body is a sight I'll never forget for as long as I live.

"Harder," he begs.

Fuck. He wants more? I thought we'd reached the limit of what he could take.

"My fucking pleasure."

I let go of his hair and push down on his upper back, forcing him onto the rug. With my cock buried in him, I spin around one hundred and eighty degrees, so that instead of fucking him from behind, I'm now facing the other direction and on top of him.

Eddie lets out a wild scream, his hands wrapping around my ankles. "Holy fucking shit that's good."

He's not wrong.

The change in angle means I'm hitting spots I wasn't able to before. I use all my strength to lift myself...before slamming into his hole, over and over until I feel that first unmistakable tingle deep in my balls.

But I'm not ready to finish yet. I promised him a good hard fuck, I'd now like to add unforgettable to that list.

I shift again until I'm somewhere in between the two positions, fucking into Eddie from the side of his body, while using my foot to push down on his head. But his ass is too low to the ground to make it work, so I hook my hands under his hips and yank his ass up until it fits just right.

He screams out in ecstasy, his hole clenching around me like a vise.

I raise my foot off him and place it down beside his face. He leans over and starts manically sucking my ankle, licking my calf, going off like a man possessed.

And that's what does it. That's what sends me over the edge. Seeing Eddie succumbing to his pleasure makes my balls tighten before I crash headfirst into a tornado of an orgasm.

I clamp both of my hands on either side of his waist and let out an almighty holler folk on the other side of the mountain can probably hear as I release my seed into the condom.

Eddie has reached around and starts coming just as my climax starts tapering off.

"Fuck!" he cries out, and as he comes, his ass starts twitching, drawing yet another orgasm out of me.

I stay in place, listening to the fire crackling away and our synced-up breathing filling the air around us.

I don't want this moment to end, but we also can't sleep here.

Closing my eyes, I pull out of Eddie's body and immediately wrap my arms around him to make up for the loss.

"Don't leave me," he begs, turning into my shoulder.

"I won't, baby. I won't." I stroke his back, staring into the fire. "You're safe with me."

After staying like that for a while, I stretch my neck and smile when I see Eddie's fallen asleep.

As quietly as I can, I pick him up and carry him into my bedroom, the smile never once leaving my face.

Dear...Name TBD

I'm so relieved you're not mad at me. And for the record, my last name is Boyd. Eddie Boyd, hence EB.

Riiight. You and your family are low-level bandits on the run. Let me guess, you've got warrants out for your arrest in three states?

And why a letter, you ask. Well, they're romantic. Texts, not so much. Besides, it's like we get to double our fun. We spend our days together, and this way, I'm thinking about you at night as well.

This also feels more intimate because I can write things I couldn't say to you in person.

Maybe that means I'm a chickenshit? Or a bastard? Either way... I'm glad you're not mad.

EB

Dear EB,

You're no chickenshit, more of a bastard. I'd insert a smiley face emoji here, but I CAN'T since we're not texting.

Boyd. I like that name...assuming it's real. Come to think of it, you sure EB stands for Eddie Boyd and not Emo Bastard? I think I like the sound of that better.

I never said my family were criminals... Just my dad. Although, technically, I guess my brothers and I are accessories.

I'm starting to like these letters, too. And I get what you mean. When I'm with you, I feel so many things. I don't even know how to describe it. It's the best feeling I've ever felt.

I wish we could spend more time together. Maybe you could sneak out once your dad's asleep? I know a cool place we can go where we can, um...do some "stuff." Maybe. Only if you want to. Only if you're ready. It's cool if you're not.

Also, you haven't come up with another fake name for me yet. Tick, tick, tick, I'm waiting...

Unsigned and nameless...

5

Eddie

My eyes flutter open. Sunlight streams into the room, and I can immediately tell that something is wrong.

It's too quiet.

No cars. No noisy neighbors banging about. No nothing. Only complete, eerie silence.

I'm lying on my side, facing a wall, when there's movement behind me. A heavy arm drapes around my middle. Harrick's hand slides into the space between the mattress and my pec. He presses his warm body against mine, just as a bird lets out a merry little chirp. It's soon joined by a chorus of other birds.

Harrick's breathing heavily, making me think he's still sleeping. His massive cock is wedged against the back of my thigh.

I asked for a dirty, rough fuck, and boy, did he come through or what, delivering the best fuck of my life. I'm not going to just feel it today, I'm probably going to feel it for the rest of the week.

I've never done that before, let myself go like that, let someone push me around and fuck me so hard, in so many different positions. But I felt completely safe the entire time. If I'd told him to stop at any stage, I know he would have.

And he never once said or did anything to make me feel like I was being used or degraded. Even when he held my head down with his foot, I found it so fucking hot and not demeaning in the slightest.

I loved every second of what we did, and I regret nothing.

I've only been with a handful of guys, but I know, with full certainty, that Harrick has ruined me for anybody else. Nothing —*no one*—will ever compare to last night.

That makes me smile for a moment until it hits me that, after today, I'll be gone and probably never see Harrick again.

I'm assuming the road will be cleared, and Harrick might drive me into town, or I'll order a ride.

Either way, what happened last night is in the past and now...now I have to get on with my life. I need to sell Pa's place, pack everything up, put his stuff into storage until I figure out what to do with it, and then get the hell off this mountain and never come back.

Michael swims into my head again, and I make a move to get up since he's literally the last person I want to be thinking about, but just then, Harrick's hand, wedged under my pec, starts to travel south.

His fingertips gently scrape the skin along my chest, my abdomen, finally resting when he reaches my dick. Somehow I'm hard despite coming four times yesterday, and as he curls his thick fingers around my length, a loud moan escapes out of me, breaking the silence.

I'm a little sore after last night but I'll be damned if I let that stop me from getting a round five out of the sexy mountain man. I wiggle my ass a little, but Harrick's strong hands grip my hips, halting the movement.

"Morning," he murmurs as he keeps me in place, while sliding down my body, positioning himself between my legs.

"Good morning."

He looks up at me. "You sore?"

I shake my head.

"Liar."

"But I didn't say anything."

"Didn't have to." He sticks his tongue out and licks a drop of pre-cum from my slit. "I can read you."

"Oh, can you now?"

"I can. I've been inside you."

"I remember...vaguely."

He grins, but it fades quickly. His stare intensifies. "This will sound so fucking crazy, but sometimes I get this feeling like..."

"Like what?"

He drops his gaze to my dick, stroking it slowly. "Forget it."

I want to press and find out what he meant to say, but the second his mouth engulfs my swollen crown, I'm a goner.

I fist the sheets with both hands as Harrick treats me to another epic blowjob, taking me right down to the base with no effort.

If I thought I'd have a tough time backing it up from last night, I quickly discover that's not the case at all.

In fact, in an embarrassingly short amount of time, he's got me on the brink.

"Getting close," I grit out.

He picks up the pace, fondling my balls between his thick fingers, making his intention clear—he wants my release.

I give it to him a few seconds later, letting out an almighty roar as my climax slams into me, thrusting my lower back off the bed and filling his mouth with my seed.

Spent, I collapse onto the bed. Harrick comes up beside me, sporting a huge grin. "Good morning."

I wipe the sweat off my forehead. "You already said that."

He chuckles. "Now I really mean it."

"In that case, now it's time for me to give you a good morning," I murmur, sliding down his body until I'm face to face with his fat cock.

"Jesus." I trace my fingers along the veins that cover his monster. "I don't know why, but I'm a sucker for a veiny cock."

Harrick grins, clasping his hands behind his head, shuffling his legs out wider. "Works for me."

And then it hits me, where this whole vein thing comes from. I'd completely forgotten.

Michael.

We never ended up having sex. We didn't get a chance. I was taken away too abruptly, but we were heading that way. I started sneaking out of the house after Pa fell asleep, and we'd meet up in this clearing in the forest not too far from our houses. It was a secluded spot, without feeling creepy.

Our nighttime meets were different from when we hung out during the day. At night, we talked less, and made out a whole lot more.

We only ever took things farther once. Lying on the ground, we unzipped our jeans and jerked each other off. I'll never forget seeing Michael's cock for the first time. How big it was, how veiny.

How strikingly similar it was to the one I'm about to blow now.

"Everything okay down there?"

"Yeah. Fine," I answer quickly, before closing my eyes, opening my mouth, and taking in as much of Harrick's dick as I can manage.

I start bobbing up and down on it, trying to keep focused on what I'm doing and nothing else. It's pretty fucked up to be blowing one guy while thinking of another, isn't it?

Pushing all thoughts of Michael out of my mind, I focus on the task at hand. Or in this case, the task in my mouth.

I take as much of Harrick's cock as I can, but there's no way the whole thing will fit down my throat. I pull out and run my tongue along all the glorious veins that line his shaft.

"You *really* have a thing for veins," he observes.

"Kinda reminds me of—"

Nope. Not finishing that sentence.

The only thing worse than thinking of someone else during sex is telling the person you're currently having sex with about it.

I start stroking madly, wanting to make Harrick feel as good as he made me feel.

His eyes roll into the back of his head. "Gonna come," he warns.

I open my mouth, jacking him off furiously, and I make it into position between his legs just in time as he starts to orgasm. The first few thick ropes land on my tongue, and I lap them up eagerly.

The next few paint my cheek, my nose, my forehead. My entire face becomes a splash zone for Harrick's gooey eruption.

"Fuck, that was good," he growls once he's done emptying himself.

He glances down, his eyes widening. "Oh, shit, sorry. Didn't realize I made such a mess."

I wave a hand. "I'm fine."

He shoots off the bed and takes off out of the bedroom. When he returns, he's holding a small white towel.

He sits down next to me on the bed. "May I?"

I give a nod, close my eyes, and tilt my head back.

The damp towel feels good against my skin as Harrick carefully wipes his cum off me.

"I've never done this before," I tell him as he wipes my forehead.

He stops. "Define this."

"Well, this." I wave at my face since I've never let a guy come on my face before. "But also what we did last night."

"It wasn't too much for you? I might've gotten a little carried away in some parts there. Don't know what came over me."

"It was a lot, but it was okay. I felt safe with you, and I...I felt free and wild and sexy."

"Good. I'm glad."

"And I've also never done this." I point at the bed.

"Never stayed over at a guy's place?" Harrick guesses.

"Nope. One time, a guy crashed at my place after a hookup. I woke up in the middle of the night and had a mini freakout. I ended up sleeping on my couch."

Harrick resumes cleaning my face. "City folk are so strange."

"Ha. Mountain people are *the worst*." I crack open an eye to see if he's offended. He doesn't seem to be, so I go on. "I once met this guy up here. Ten years ago. He had long blond hair, down way past his shoulders and he...he was my first love. And my first heartbreak."

Harrick stops drying my face. He's sporting a huge frown

and looks...anguished. As if my words are somehow wounding *him*, and not me.

He gets up abruptly. "You're all done. Mind if I shower first?"

"Uh, no. Go for it."

He runs out of the room so fast, like his ass is on fire.

"That was weird," I grumble as I walk over and pick up the discarded clothes he lent me yesterday and put them on.

With the shower still running, I meander into the living room. Bright sunlight fills the room and the fire is almost out. It really is a new day. Time for me to be thinking about making plans to head off.

I walk over to the window in the dining room and take a look outside. Didn't get a chance to see much yesterday what with all the rain, but it's beautiful here. The cabin is secluded so there's nothing but thick, dense forest surrounding it. I may hate the mountains, but I can still appreciate the beauty of nature.

As I make my way back from the window, I accidentally bump the table, knocking some of the papers stacked neatly in the corner onto the floor.

"Crap."

I crouch down and gather them up. They seem to be mostly official business papers, so I don't look at them in any detail. I'm not one to pry.

I go to grab the last piece of paper on the floor, and I choke on my breath.

This isn't an official business letter...

It's *mine*. One of my letters I wrote to Michael all those years ago.

Right at that moment, Harrick enters the room. He stalks over to the dining table and glares at me, looming over me with his jaw clenched.

I stand up slowly, even though my heart is racing at full throttle, and lift the letter to show him. "Who the hell are you, and why the fuck do you have this letter?"

6

Harrick

This can't be happening. This *can't* be happening.

But it is.

The undeniable truth of it all slammed into me in the bedroom, when Eddie told me about his first love.

Up here in the mountains.

A decade ago.

The guy with long, blond hair down to his shoulders.

That was me.

It *has* to be. There was no one else in Thickehead at that time who matched that description.

Helps explain Eddie's thing for veins, too. I remember the only time we did anything more than kissing. A side-by-side jack off. When he saw my cock for the first time, he was mesmerized. Maybe that's where he's got it from?

Combined, it was all the confirmation I needed—this Eddie *is* my Eddie.

A cold shower has done nothing to quell the million thoughts whirling around in my head... Or the rage simmering in my veins.

For abandoning me without so much as a goodbye letter.

For never coming back.

For moving on with his life and not giving me a second thought, discarding me like I didn't matter. Like I was just some meaningless summertime fling. A chance for a confused kid, who didn't know who he was or what he wanted to do with his life, to hang out and experiment with the wild mountain boy.

Fuck him for doing that to me.

I glare at Eddie, then shift my focus to the letter he's holding. I'd been moving some stuff around and forgot to put it away.

Then I realize...*he* doesn't know it's *me* yet.

I look down at my feet, take a deep breath, then slowly lift my head, my eyes connecting with his. That's the one piece of the puzzle I can't figure out. My Eddie's eyes were brown. This Eddie's eyes are blue. What gives? Does eye color change? Is that even possible?

"What's your surname?" I demand.

"No, no, no." Eddie shoves past me with a huff and starts pacing the length of the living room. "You don't get to ask the questions around here. I do."

He stops in his tracks and squints at me, like he doesn't know who he's looking at. "Answer me, dammit. Who. Are. *You*?"

His voice rumbles in frustration, and I'm pissed, too. A little confused, but mainly pissed. If he is who I'm ninety-nine percent sure he is, I have a meteor-sized bone to pick with him.

But my anger will have to wait, because despite him hurting me like no one ever has, there's a tiny part of me, a part of me that had died, and I thought was gone forever, that's stirring back to life. A part of me that feels an awful lot like hope, a throwback remnant from the time when my Eddie was able to draw emotions like that out of me.

So I stare straight into Eddie's questioning blue eyes, blow out a breath, and say, "I'm Princess."

He lets out a shocked gasp and rocks back on his heels. I lunge forward, convinced he's about to faint.

But he doesn't.

And in my haste, I overshoot my target.

The next thing I know, my large frame is crashing down on top of him and then we're *both* plunging toward the floor.

Dear Princess,

There? You like the new name? I think it suits you. You know, 'cause you've got long hair and how you kinda rule the mountains. Like a boss royal.

Side note: If you're a princess, then that means I'm a prince and...I like that for me. (See what you mean about not being able to add in smiley face emojis. I could really do with one right about now).

Still can't tell if you're pulling my leg about your family or not. I casually mentioned something to Pa about your dad when I got in today, and he got super mad and shut the conversation down straightaway. Has your dad ever mentioned my dad? Do the two of them have beef or something?

I'm down for sneaking out but...takes a deep breath, prays you don't judge me...I'm still a virgin. (Sooo much easier writing this than saying it to your face, by the way).

That said, I do want to do "stuff" with you, but maybe we can take it slow? We have the whole summer. I'm not going back home for another five weeks.

Your EB (Emo Bastard - yep, I'm officially claiming it)

Dear Emo Bastard,

That does have a nice ring to it. I'm a genius!

Um, Princess. Princess! Princess??!!

That's a...choice. You realize that if you're basing my nickname off my hair and the fact I live in the mountains, you could've chosen Tarzan. But hey, if it's what you want—and you swear to tell NO ONE—then I'll go along with it. But only because you have such a beautiful smile...when you're not being all emo and angsty, that is.

Unlikely that there's anything going on between my dad and yours. Dad mostly keeps to himself, doubt your father is even on his radar.

I would never judge you for being a virgin. Thank you for sharing that with me. I want you to know you can tell me anything, and I'll never make you feel bad. Promise.

In the interest of full disclosure, I'm not a virgin. I've had sex with two guys. But it's only ever been a physical thing. You...you've found a way to touch me, to open my heart and make me FEEL things. So many things. I suck at describing it, but it's like there's an explosion in my heart every time I see you. You do something to me that makes me feel life isn't as shitty and bad. That there is a bright future for me. For us!

You're my Emo Bastard, and I hope you always will be.

Your...Princess (slowly getting used to it)

7

Eddie

My back meets the wooden floor with a loud and painful thud. But that's not the worst of it.

I've still got two hundred and thirty pounds of mountain man hurtling toward me. Harrick manages to think faster than I seem capable of and sticks his arms out, bracing for impact.

It works.

Kinda.

He still falls on top of me, but his arms cop the brunt of his weight, saving me from getting crushed under his body, because trust me, this would not be the good type of crushed. It'd be the type that involves broken bones and paramedics.

Harrick's body is on top of me, the tip of his nose inches away from mine. His warm breath cascades over my face, and he stares at me, as darkly and intensely as ever.

I try to clear my head and pretend I'm seeing him for the first time.

Are they Michael's eyes? Could they be? Or is this guy some psycho who goes around pretending to be someone else? Someone who I loved ten years ago and have never gotten over.

Maybe he is Michael...but then the beard, his hefty frame, his whole silent vibe... How is this mountain man my Princess?

He's not. He can't be.

Can he?

Now that I've gotten over the initial shock, anger burns through my chest. I slam my palms into Harrick's chest to shove him the fuck off me, the swirling emotions inside me erupting.

He doesn't move, like he doesn't even register the impact. It infuriates me even more, and I'm about to give this asshole a piece of my mind when one solitary word rolls out of his lips.

"Boyd."

I freeze.

He doesn't elaborate.

A moment passes.

His eyes fall away from mine, and I turn everything over in my mind.

He has my letter.

He said he lived on the mountain years ago, and he's returned.

He knows my surname.

"How?" I force out. "How are you my Princess?"

"My name's not Michael," he begins in a low, gravelly tone. "It never was. My dad really was a criminal. Wasn't kidding about that. We were on the run, hiding out in the mountains until the heat was off."

I reach out and touch the end of a loose strand of his hair. "Your hair is shorter."

"It is. Not as short as it was when I was in the military. I'm growing it back."

"It was lighter, too."

"It goes lighter in summer."

"So, it's really...you?"

He brushes his finger down the side of my face, his expression unreadable but a little softer and less intense than it was a few moments ago. "It is."

"And Harrick is your real name? You're not still on the run, are you?"

A tiny smile. "Real name. No longer on the run. Promise."

"Oh, you promise, do you?" I retort, a receding flame of anger flaring up. "Like I'm not just processing the fact that you lied to me about everything ten years ago. That the person I fell in love with for the first time, the whole experience I had with you, that everything about that was fake. What was it? Just some silly game to you? I was some dumb city kid going through an emo phase that you could toy with?"

"Nothing about us was fake," he growls. "And you're one to fucking talk. You deserted me in the middle of the night without so much as a letter to tell me you were leaving."

"I didn't desert you. I was taken. Dad must've found our letters. He called my mom, and she came to get me and take me back to the city. I didn't know what was happening until she was there, yelling at me to pack my stuff so we could go. I didn't have time to write you a letter. It broke my heart having to leave you."

"Broke your heart, huh? And you were so damn heartbroken that you never came back, huh?"

"I came back." I squeeze my eyes shut, breathing through the pain. "But you were gone."

Our chests are pounding against each other. It's not easy arguing with someone when they're literally lying on top of you, especially when it's releasing years and years of pent-up emotions and hurt.

"Can you get off me please?" I whimper. "I'm starting to feel nauseous."

Harrick rolls off me, and I sit upright. He crosses his legs, remaining a few feet away from me on the floor.

An awkward silence hangs between us.

"Your eyes."

I shake my head. "What about them?"

"They were brown."

"I was using colored contact lenses. I went all in on the emo thing, remember?"

"Right... When did you come back for me?"

"A few months later."

"A few *months*?"

The raw anguish in his voice makes my chest hurt.

Unable to bring myself to tell him what I need to while looking at him, I turn away. It's still too damn painful, even after all this time.

"Mom didn't take me back home. She took me to a conversion clinic."

I take a break, willing myself on. *I'm strong. I can say this. He deserves to know the truth.* "One of those places where they try to 'cure the gay' out of you."

"But you were eighteen."

"*Almost* eighteen. Technically, I was a minor for a few more weeks, and apparently, that was good enough for the place I got locked up in. It was...a nightmare."

"I can't even imagine. Eddie, I'm so sorry that happened to you."

"I was released after three months. Borrowed a friend's car and came back here right away. Had a huge blow up with Pa. And then to top it all off, he told me you'd joined the military. I was devastated on so many levels."

I start crying.

The thing about me is I'm not a pretty crier. My face goes all red and splotchy, my nose gets snotty, and I blubber like an idiot.

None of that stops Harrick from coming over and crouching beside me. "Can I hug you?" I hear him ask over a sob.

I manage a weak yes, and it's enough for him to scooch closer and wrap me up in his big strong arms. I'm so caught up in the trauma of what happened, what my mother did to me, that it hasn't really sunk in who's hugging me.

Princess.

All this time, I was convinced that he'd taken off and not given me a second thought. I never considered that he'd feel I abandoned him. How fucking awful. No wonder he snapped back at me.

My time at the conversion camp messed me up, and it took years of therapy for me to work through it all. The summer I spent with Michael/Princess/Harrick got caught up in all of that. Another piece of baggage I had to resolve and try to move on from.

But it never worked.

I pull back slightly so I can see Harrick's face, mentally superimposing it onto the face I remember staring into all those years ago. I take advantage of a break in my tears to whisper, "I never stopped loving you."

His dark eyes water. "I never stopped loving you, either."

And that brings on the waterworks yet again.

Harrick holds me close, his strong arms and warm body providing the comfort I need so desperately right now. My tears keep pouring out of me.

"I'm sorry," I say, sitting up and wiping away the tears.

Harrick and I both look down at his shirt at the same time. It's soaked through.

"For that," I joke weakly. "But mainly for the pain me leaving caused you. I had no idea. All this time, I was under the impression that you were the one who moved on. That I was making a bigger deal out of what we had than I should have. That you didn't really care about me."

"Oh, baby."

Harrick brings me in closer, and I rest the side of my face against his shoulder. His fingers massage my scalp. "I'm still in shock this is really happening."

I sniffle." It's a lot to take in. You're so...different."

"I am." There's a heaviness to his tone. "Life has changed me."

I peer up at him. "For the better?"

He narrows his eyes. "TBD... But I have received some very good news recently."

I crack a tiny grin. "Care to elaborate?"

He lifts my chin, then brings his lips to mine. We're both smiling as we kiss, and suddenly, we're transported back ten years in time. We're not two men kissing on the floor of a mountain cabin, we're two young guys, with their feet dangling off a cliff, the sun setting in front of them, sharing that first precious, tender moment together.

"God, how I've missed you, Princess," I murmur against his lips.

Harrick chuckles. "I'm officially petitioning to change that in favor of Tarzan."

"I thought you liked Princess."

"I was starting to get used to it...for you. But if I was a princess then, that means I'd have to be a queen now. And..."

"I'm the queen in this relationship."

A huge smile blooms on his face. "Yeah. You are. You're my queen. And my king. And my fucking everything."

"Even if I'm not the confused, angsty emo kid I tried to be? You sure that's not who you're in love with?"

"I fell in love with the person beneath the clothes and the hair and the...fucking contact lenses. I fell in love with your soul, Eddie. No one has ever made me feel the way you do, and I'm feeling it right now. Sitting here on the freaking floor with you. This is my idea of heaven. I wouldn't want to be anywhere else or with anyone else."

I take him in, this strong, gorgeous, genuinely kind-hearted mountain man, and smile.

One of his eyebrows lifts. "What?"

"Nothing. It's just..." I start to say softly through a chuckle. "You're talking. Actually, no. You're blabbering. Like, nonstop. How you used to."

"Yeah... I am." He seems a little taken aback, but then he shrugs. "Guess you bring it out in me, Princess."

"Oh. *I'm* the princess now, am I?"

"Only if you'd like to be."

"Maybe I would." My hand slides between our bodies, stopping when it lands on his heavy bulge. "On one condition."

A carnal look ignites his eyes. "And what would that be?"

I lean forward and give the thick column of his neck one slow, delicious lick. When I reach his ear, I hum. "I want you to treat me like a princess, but fuck me like a cheap whore. Just like you did last night."

"You got it...*Princess*."

8

Harrick

I roll off Eddie and onto the hard wooden floor beside him. I swipe a hand through my damp hair, exhausted after giving him the rough and dirty dicking he requested.

"Was that the nasty sex you were looking for?" I pant.

I glance over at him. I fucked him so hard, so thoroughly, so brutally, I turned his tears of pain into tears of ecstasy. He's totally blissed out, lying there, sweaty, with his mouth gaping open, sucking in oxygen.

"So good," he eventually croaks, then turns his head.

Our eyes meet.

It's such a weird feeling. I now *know* he's my Eddie, but his eyes were different back then. I'm going to need some time to get used to it, to reconcile the two Eddies into one.

Hopefully, this time, we'll get the time that was stolen from us a decade ago.

We lie there for a few minutes, naked on the floor, just staring at each other.

My mind revisits everything he told me—about his father finding the letters, his mom taking him to that god-awful place...him coming back for me as soon as he could.

"You're so strong," I whisper, as I delicately brush the side of his face with the backs of my fingers. "For surviving what you went through. Those places can fuck people up for life."

"You're strong, too." He clasps his fingers around my hand, brings it to his lips, and peppers it with sweet kisses. "Can't even begin to imagine the horror you saw on the battlefield. That messes with people for the rest of their lives, too."

"It's why I moved up here. To get away from everything."

Eddie keeps my fingers pressed to his lips, but he's stopped kissing them. He's thinking... His eyes might be a different color, but I can recognize that much.

"Who do you think we are?"

"I...don't understand."

"I still feel like I haven't figured myself out yet. I'm not an emo teenager anymore, and I have learned some things about myself. I have a great job, friends, a life, a car up until recently, but I still don't feel like I'm there yet, you know? Like I'm a complete and fully formed adult."

"Is anyone?" I thread my fingers through his. "I don't think anyone ever gets there. That's not the point of life."

"What is then?"

"The point of life?"

He nods.

"I just came about sixty billion gallons, and you're asking me a question that humankind has pondered since the dawn of time?"

A beat of silence, and then he grins. "I am."

"Maybe we don't have to figure it out?" I suggest, because I'm pretty sure he won't let me off without answering. "Both life and who we are. Maybe we're just meant to experience the stuff we go through, try our best to be good people, and live as happily as we can."

That grin is back on his lips.

"Are you laughing at me for rambling so much?"

"I'm not laughing. I'm enjoying it. Maybe you're not a silent mountain man, after all?"

"I'm not the wild, long-haired kid anymore, either. I can assure you of that."

"So who is Harrick... Shit. I don't even know your last name. Or your middle name. Wait. Do you have a middle name?"

"I don't."

"And what's your last name?"

"Tarzan. Harrick Tarzan."

Eddie rolls his eyes. "Bullshit."

"I'm not kidding."

"It is not. No one has a name like that."

"I do."

"Prove it."

"You want me to show you my driver's license?"

"Yes."

With an exaggerated sigh, I peel myself off the floor and walk over to the side table in the entryway to fetch my wallet.

I return to Eddie, who's sitting up now, watching his face as I slide the license out of my wallet. I rejoin him on the floor and make it look like I'm about to hand it over, then I pull it away at the last minute, twirling it between my fingers.

"What do I get if I'm right? If my surname really is Tarzan?"

He eyes me suspiciously. "What do you want?"

"I'm pretty satisfied with what we just did." As evidenced by the cum stains on the floor all around us. "I'd be happy with doing that a few times a week."

"Silly mountain man. You should've asked for something better." Eddie leans over and snatches the license from my fingers. "You're going to get that anyway."

Before he looks to check what my name really is, he tilts his head, his teeth gnawing into his lower lip. "And what do I get if you're bullshitting me?"

"What do *you* want?"

"Us," he answers firmly and with no hesitation.

"What about us?"

"A chance for us to make it work."

"I... I can't live in the city, Eddie. I'm sorry."

"That's okay. I can move here."

"What about your job?"

"I already work from home three days of the week. It should be fine. And if it's not, I can get another job."

"What about your friends? Your apartment? Your life?"

He frowns. "Are you trying to put me off? Is this not what you want?"

"Of course it's what I want. Not a day has gone by these past ten years that I haven't thought about you, wondering what it would be like if we'd had the rest of the summer. If, after that, we could've gone somewhere and started a life together."

"So why are you throwing all these roadblocks in my face now?"

"Because it's a lot to ask. What if you give everything up to move here and be with me, and at some point down the track, you end up resenting me for it? Or what if you hate it? This life isn't for everyone. Which reminds me, don't you hate the mountains, City Boy?"

"I hate what the mountains reminded me of. Pa betraying me and losing you. The mountains themselves are fine. I have nothing against trees and fresh air and all that nature stuff."

"Glad to hear it."

"I'm serious, Harrick. Losing you has been the biggest regret of my life. You could be right. I could hate it here, but I promise you this, I'd rather try and know for sure, than walk away and live with what-ifs for the rest of my life. That sucks way more. Believe me."

"Oh, trust me. I know all about that."

His eyes dart to the license, then back to me. "So, do you agree? If I win and your surname isn't Tarzan..." He tries to keep a straight face as he says it. "Then we become a thing?"

I scratch my chest and pretend to think about it. "Would we have to make it Instagram official?"

"Now is not the time to be funny, mister." He swats my chest. "Do we have a deal?"

"Yes. We have a deal."

"Good."

He starts to slowly lift the license higher, and I swear, I'm enjoying this way too much. I actually think he's not entirely sure at this stage. I'm going to lord this moment over him for the rest of our lives.

He looks down, then up at me. Then down at the license and up one more time. He tosses me an adorable smile that makes my cold, brutish heart melt.

"Duncan. Harrick Duncan."

"Guilty as charged."

He pushes forward. I brace my hands around his waist and stare into the face, the eyes, of the only man I've ever loved. "It's a pleasure to meet you."

"You wanna talk about pleasure?" He licks the side of my face. "The pleasure is about to be all mine."

We kiss.

Hungrily, passionately, desperately.

I can't even say that I've waited for this moment because I didn't ever conceive that it would come to be. I thought my Eddie was gone forever and that I was destined to be alone for the rest of my days. Because the only thing I knew for certain was that no one—*no one*—could even come close to matching what he did to me, how he made me feel, all those years ago.

Eddie and I spend the rest of the day having filthy sex. We only take a break long enough to move onto the sheepskin rug and for me to get the fire going again.

"I can't believe this is real," I murmur as I'm buried to the hilt inside Eddie's tight channel.

"Me, either. Fuck. I hope it's not a dream."

I thrust into him, and he bucks off the rug.

"Yep. Okay. Definitely not a dream," he rasps.

"I love you so much, Eddie. I missed you. Every single day."

"I missed you every day, too."

We both sigh at the same time. I stop pumping, but stay inside him. Gently, I reposition myself so that my body covers his, mindful of not putting all my weight on him.

We're flush together.

I can feel his heart beating.

The rise and fall of his chest against mine.

I love this man.

My Eddie.

And I'm going to spend every day, for as many days as I'm blessed to have on this earth, telling him, showing him, how special he is and how much he means to me.

9

Eddie

We pass out at some point after our fourth, maybe fifth round of sex. I lost count, lost track of time, lost sense of anything that wasn't Harrick or me.

I stir, letting out a yawn as I look up. The fire's still going, but it's dark out. Harrick's lying behind me, just like he was this morning when I woke up in his bed.

It's been a wild day and a half, that's for sure.

Did I mean what I told him? That I want to move up here and start a life with him. You bet I did. I've never wanted anything more.

We had our future stolen from us once before, and I'm not going to let that happen again. Whatever it takes, I'm going to do it if it means being with the man I'm meant to be with.

My soulmate.

Like he said so beautifully himself, Harrick loves me for who I am. He sees past all the surface-level stuff, and even though I don't know who I am, he loves me anyway.

I feel the same way about him, whether he stays the strong silent man he's become, or if he revives some of his personality traits from his past. I'll love him no matter what.

"I can *feel* you thinking," Harrick murmurs, pressing a kiss to my shoulder.

"That's not me thinking you're feeling. It's probably your cum from when you blew on my ass before."

He lets out a raspy chuckle, and I turn around so I'm facing him. "I love you, Tarzan."

He smiles approvingly. "I love you, too, Princess."

"I have so many questions."

"What about?"

"Your dad. Your brothers. Your military life. How you're really doing."

"Let me tackle them in reverse order."

"Okay."

"I'm doing really fucking good now."

"But what about before I showed up and rocked your world...again. Were you doing okay? Be honest with me."

He blows out a breath. "I was okay, but not great. I tried to convince myself that living alone was the better option. That people only hurt you. And, while that is true, people can cause you pain, they can also bring unimaginable joy. You have to figure out whether that's a risk you're willing to take."

"Is it a risk *you're* willing to take? With me?"

He runs his finger under my jaw. "That's the thing. It doesn't feel scary with you. Nothing could top the devastation I felt when you left. I, *we*, have been given a second chance. Our first proper shot. No way I'm not going to take it."

"That's exactly how I feel. It's a big decision to move up here and be with you, and I know it won't be hunky-dory all the time, but I'm not afraid. I trust you. I trusted you super fast, even before I knew who you really were."

"Maybe your soul knew who I was?"

"Nah. I just saw your bulge and thought there's no way I can pass up an enormous cock."

Harrick smiles. "Shut up."

"Okay, next thing."

"Military life?"

I nod.

His smile fades, replaced by a deep frown. "Mind if I take a raincheck on that one? I will tell you, but just not now, if that's okay?"

"Of course it is. Someone once wrote something in a letter to me, saying that I could tell them anything and they'd never make me feel bad for it. The same applies to you, for anything you want to tell me, or *not* tell me. I'll never judge, and I'll never pressure you."

Harrick takes my hands in his and lifts them to his lips. "Thank you. That means a lot."

"But I am dying to know about your family. Because for reals, I thought you were pulling my leg about your dad being a criminal and you guys being on the run."

"It was all true. Dad's still kicking about. He's somewhere in Mexico, last time we spoke. I think he's finally settling down...a bit."

"And what about your brothers? You have two, right, and they're older than you?"

"Correct. They both live on the mountain. You'll get to meet them."

"Are you guys close?"

"Annoyingly so."

"Are they married? Kids?"

"No and no... Any more questions? Geez, I feel like I'm getting grilled over here."

"Sorry, sorry. I'm just overexcited. We have so much to catch up on."

"We do. And we have the rest of our lives to do it, Princess."

I beam. "Is it wrong how much I love you calling me that?"

"Not at all. Is it wrong how much I love calling you that?"

We laugh, then we make out like teenagers for a while.

Because we can.

Because no one is going to tear us apart ever again.

There are still practical life things to work out. Like calling insurance about my car. Having to sell Pa's old place. Dealing with the practicalities of moving from the city to the mountains and getting used to small-town life. It'll be an adjustment for sure, but so much of my hatred of the mountains came down to the bad association I had with them.

But I also had lots of good memories, too, both from my childhood with Pa and from the summer with Mich—Harrick. And now I have an opportunity to create a whole bunch of new, amazing memories.

"I'm happier than I can describe."

"Me, too, Princess."

We start kissing again.

I never thought it was possible for two human beings to be so connected to one another, but when it feels as good as it does between Harrick and me, I *know* we'll get through whatever challenges come our way, and everything will work out just fine.

Now that we've found each other again, nothing is going to stand in our way.

~

Want more mountain man yummy-ness?

Flip the page for a sneak peek of The Curious Mountain Man!

SNEAK PEEK AT THE CURIOUS MOUNTAIN MAN

I'm a nerdy, neurodivergent librarian who lives a quiet life in the mountains. While out birdwatching one day, I stumble upon a giant of a mountain man bathing in the lake.

Naked.

I manage to run away, hoping he didn't see me.

And then he shows up at my library.

Something about him lures me in. Sure, he's tall, bearded, and insanely gorgeous, but there's a gentle curiosity in his eyes. And when he looks at me, it's like he's trying to understand me...

Orrrr maybe I'm imagining it.

Yeah, that's probably it. I mean, why would a handsome, barrel-chested lumberjack like Branum be interested in a Mr. Plain and Boring like me?

. . .

Chapter 1

Branum

My skin prickles... Eyes are on me.

I can *feel* it.

My survival instincts are well-honed.

A childhood spent on the run with a father hiding from the law, needing to keep a low profile, constantly keeping a lookout over my shoulder, has equipped me with a sixth sense for these things.

I kick off my hiking shoes and peel the shirt off my sweaty back, dropping it onto the jagged edge of a boulder.

Lifting my arms overhead for a much-needed stretch after a five-hour hike, I stare out at the river that runs through the back of my fifty-acre property.

I'm moving normally. Acting natural.

I'm not sensing danger, just...*a presence*.

And if someone has trespassed onto my land and is watching me, they're about to get more than they bargained for.

I unzip my shorts and push them down my legs and step out of them. Then I hook my thumbs into the waistband of my briefs and do the same.

I stand to full height, soaking in the rays as they stream down on my naked body.

I'm the middle child of three brothers, but I'm much larger than Harrick and Marsh. Running my timber yard not only keeps me plenty busy, it also means I'm in pretty decent shape. Good thing, too, because while my metabolism may be slowing down in my thirties, my appetite sure ain't.

I turn my head from side to side, slowly, like I'm simply taking in the rugged landscape and beautiful tall pine trees, not trying to clock from which direction I'm being spied on.

I click my jaw to clear my ears, on the hunt for any sound, any indication, to confirm I'm not alone.

Nothing.

But that doesn't mean there's no one here, it just means they're good at being stealthy.

I climb onto the giant boulder and curl my toes over the edge before I dive in. The cool blue water sets off a tingling sensation as it washes over my heated skin.

I love being in nature. Sky, water, mountains. The elements ground me and make me come alive at the same time, remind me of what's real. If it's an outdoor activity—hiking, swimming, fishing, you name it—I'm in.

I swim underwater for as long as I can hold my breath before bobbing to the surface. I flip onto my back and float for a while, gazing up at the endlessly blue sky.

The sun beats down on parts of my body that are breaching the surface of the water—my face, my toes, my shoulders, my cock.

I reach down and readjust my dick, resting it flat along my stomach.

It starts to thicken.

I'm not an exhibitionist by any means, but there's no harm in toying with my anonymous onlooker is there? If they don't like what they're seeing, they're free to leave and trespass on someone else's land whenever they want. No one's holding a gun to their head.

After all, *they're* invading *my* privacy.

I run my fingers along the underside of my exposed cock, and as it grows, it rises into the air. A droplet of pre-cum pearls at the slit.

I lift my head so that my ears are fully out of the water.

Still nothing but the sound of the river flowing and birds chirping.

And then... A crackle, like someone stepping on a twig or fallen branch.

My pulse accelerates, but I don't let it show.

It could be an animal, or if it is a human visitor, it's most likely a lost tourist. Even though I live on the outer edges of Thickehead, the charming mountain town attracts a swarm of year-round tourists to the region.

There's a hiking trail a few miles away from my property line. Maybe someone took a wrong turn?

I stop floating and stand in the waist-deep water, swiping my hands through my slick hair, brushing it off my face.

I make my way toward the water's edge, taking long, deep strides, letting my eyes roam through the thick forest, trying to catch a glimpse of whoever is there.

I haul myself up onto the giant rock I dove in from and pat myself dry with my T-shirt. I bend down to gather my clothes when I hear a sound to my right.

Footsteps.

Dropping everything, I race off in the direction of the sound. Yep, somebody is definitely on my property.

I give chase.

The thing about running barefoot in a forest is that it kills your feet. As keen as I am to find out who my intruder is, a few prickly twigs spike painfully into my soles, quickly putting an end to things.

Dammit. They're getting away.

I scan my surroundings, hoping to catch a glimpse of whoever it is. Suddenly, in the gap between two massive trees, a person comes into my line of sight.

They're hightailing it out of here as fast as they can, but for a few brief seconds, I get a clear, unobstructed view.

It's a man.

Wearing a navy blue shirt with a black backpack flung over his shoulders.

But it's not what he's wearing that captures my attention.

No.

The detail my eyes fixate on is the mop of red curls on top of his head.

I have my answer. I know who my unexpected guest is.

He slips out of view, but I stand there, grinning like an idiot.

A naked idiot.

But it looks like this naked idiot is about to pay a visit to the local library.

ABOUT CASEY COX

Casey Cox is an Australian MM romance author whose work includes the hugely popular *VET SHOP BOYS* series.

Casey loves spending time at the beach and is the proud paw-rent to two utterly adorable French Bulldogs - Ralphie and Lilly.

For more information about Casey, please visit - **www.caseycoxbooks.com**

Printed in Great Britain
by Amazon